KT-479-944

GRuBtoWN taLes
Book Four

The WRoNg
ENd of the Dog

or

The Pedal-Bin Pelican

Cardiff Libraries
www.cardiff.gov.uk/libraries

Llyfrgelloedd Cae
www.cae.dydd.gov.uk/llyfr

ACC. No: 05028334

A bit about the author

Philip Ardagh is the award-winning author of the Eddie Dickens adventures, currently in over 30 languages. He wrote BBC Radio's first truly interactive radio drama, collaborated with Sir Paul McCartney on his first children's book and is a 'regularly irregular' reviewer of children's books for the *Guardian*. Married with a son, he divides his time between Tunbridge Wells and Grubtown, where he cultivates his impressive beard.

Other children's books by Philip Ardagh published by Faber & Faber

GRuBtoWN taLes
Stinking Rich and Just Plain Stinky
The Year That It Rained Cows
The Far From Great Escape
The Great Pasta Disaster (*World Book Day Special Book*)

FICTION FOR 8+
The Eddie Dickens Trilogy
Awful End
Dreadful Acts
Terrible Times
The Further Adventures of Eddie Dickens
Dubious Deeds
Horrendous Habits
Final Curtain
Unlikely Exploits
The Fall of Fergal
Heir of Mystery
The Rise of the House of McNally

High In The Clouds
with Paul McCartney & Geoff Dunbar

NON-FICTION
The Hieroglyphs Handbook
Teach Yourself Ancient Egyptian
The Archaeologist's Handbook
The Insider's Guide To Digging Up The Past
Did Dinosaurs Snore?
100½ Questions about Dinosaurs Answered
Why Are Castles Castle-Shaped?
100½ Questions about Castles Answered

GRuBtoWN taLes
Book Four

The WRoNg
ENd of the Dog

or

The Pedal-Bin Pelican

by Philip Ardagh

Illustrated by Jim Paillot

ff

faber and faber

For my brother.
It's about time he had another dedication

First published in 2010
by Faber and Faber Limited
Bloomsbury House
74–77 Great Russell Street
London
WC1B 3DA

Typeset by Faber and Faber Limited
Printed in England by CPI Bookmarque, Croydon

All rights reserved
© Philip Ardagh, 2010
Illustrations © Jim Paillot, 2010
Worm illustration on page 3 and 'blank' illustration on page 49
© Philip Ardagh, 2010

The right of Philip Ardagh to be identified as author of this work
has been asserted in accordance with Section 77 of the Copyright,
Designs and Patents Act 1988

This is a work of fiction. Other than those clearly in the public
domain, all characters, businesses, places, properties, products,
organisations and even Grubtown itself are figments of the author's
imagination (with the possible exception of himself). Any similarities
to existing entities, past or present, are purely coincidental and
should not be inferred.

A CIP record for this book
is available from the British Library

ISBN 978–0–571–24792–9

2 4 6 8 10 9 7 5 3 1

A bit about Grubtown

You won't find Grubtown on any maps. The last time any mapmakers were sent anywhere near the place they were found a week later wearing nothing but pages from a telephone directory, and calling for their mothers. It's certainly a town and certainly grubby – except for the squeaky clean parts – but everything else we know about the place comes from Beardy Ardagh, town resident and author of these tales.

GRuBtoWN taLes were made possible through the participation of the following people, animals and organisations:

THE GRUBTOWN
CHAMBER OF COMMERCE

THE GRUBTOWN
CHAMBER OF
HORRORS

THE OFFICE
*of the Mayor
of Grubtown*

OFFAL'S
SUNBEDS

THE SHED
*of the Mayor
of Grubtown*

*The Mayor
of Grubtown
Himself*

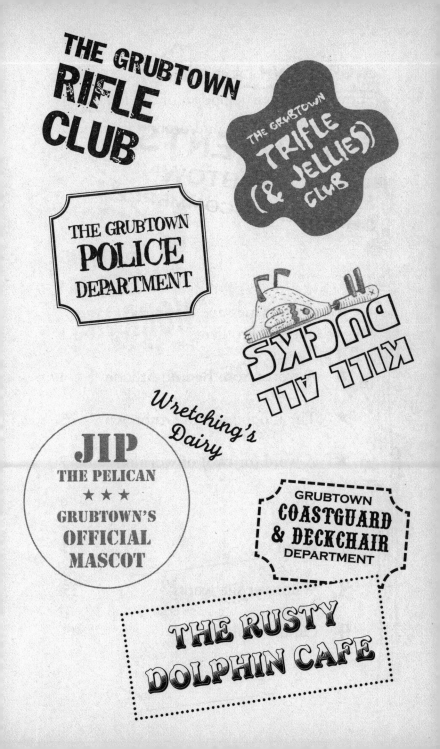

CONTENTS

A short message about the author's brother

My brother, Smoothy-Chin Ardagh, doesn't have a beard and he doesn't live in Grubtown. (He currently lives in another seaside town called Beg's Hill Uncy.) He does, however, read all my books. I don't mean that he reads the books I get out of Grubtown Lending Library & Carpet Cleaners or the ones I 'borrow' from Limpet Stair-Rail's bookstore on Crimp Street (which I always put back if I remember). I mean that he reads all the books I've *written*, including these GRuBtoWN taLes.

A question he often asks me is, 'Why are you sitting on my lap?', to which I reply: 'Because you're more comfortable than any of my chairs.'

1

This is a lie, because – unlike me – he is very thin with knobbly joints, but sitting on him does save wear and tear on my furniture.

The other day, he also asked me, 'Does the Fox family play a big part in this latest book?'

The answer was 'No,' but he didn't believe me.

Beardy Ardagh.

Grubtown

A worm from Beardy Ardagh

I'm on the lookout for the early bird!

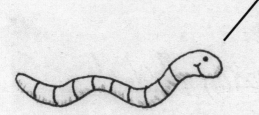

*Author's note: I think this should read 'A **word** from Beardy Ardagh'.*

The inhabitants of Grubtown

At the back of the book (starting on page 119), you'll find a list of some of the people who live in Grubtown, including Jilly Cheeter and Mango Claptrap. The people don't appear in any particular order. I was thinking of putting the people I like most at the beginning and the ones I like least at the end, or in order of their height, or of those most likely to be a disappointment to their families in the next six months. Then I decided not to. It's just a list.

Live with it.

A word (or two) of warning

L ook out!

Chapter One
Slip-up!

When the movie star Tawdry Hipbone slipped on some apple peel and landed on her million-dollar bottom with a thump, it was only Bunty Fox who sniggered. Miss Hipbone was there to promote her new film called *For the Love of Ducks II*. In it, she plays Pristine Hindrance, a woodcutter's daughter who – after an accident with a log – finds true happiness (and lots of pond weed) by being kind to ducks.

The sniggering Bunty Fox hates ducks. You want evidence? She and her husband own a shop called KILL ALL DUCKS. Proof enough that she's not a big fan of them, I'd say.

A large crowd had gathered outside SMOKY'S – Grubtown's one and only cinema – to greet Miss Hipbone for the Special Charity Gala Performance of the film, and the police were out in big numbers: both Chief Grabby Hanson and Sergeant Constable Gelatine were there, along with Gelatine's nephew, Officer Mustard Tripwire. (Yup, it was just the three of them but they were wearing *great* uniforms. No one on Earth could look more like a chief of police than Grabby Hanson in his full-dress (special-occasion) police uniform. When off-duty he could get a job playing chiefs of police in films and on television if he wanted to.)

Mayor Flabby Gomez had provided a short length of red carpet to cover the distance from Miss Hipbone's big and shiny – and ridiculously long – car to the door of the cinema. (He kept different lengths of carpet in the seven-storey-high garden shed he was living in whilst knitting a new home.)

He had instructed Hetty Glue-Pen, **SMOKY'S** manager and projectionist, to set up two microphones just outside the cinema doors: one for him to give his speech into and one for Tawdry Hipbone to say nice stuff about him and Grubtown and, of course, about *For the Love of Ducks II*.

Mayor Gomez had been practising his speech for over a week, but now it looked like it might not happen. The movie star had slipped on the apple peel, between the limo and theatre steps, before he'd even had a chance to say, 'Greetings, fellow citizens of Grubtown!'

He shouted, 'Blimey!' instead.

There was a great big gasp from the great big crowd . . . and just that one snigger from Mrs Fox, of course. Chief of Police Grabby

Hanson leapt forward to the distressed Miss Hipbone and helped her to her feet with one hand while rummaging through her glittery handbag with the other. He managed to slip into his pocket a small gold-framed mirror and an unopened packet of Hotty Mintettes (*The*

little mints with the big bite). Grabby's not called 'Grabby' for nothing.

Constable Gelatine, meanwhile, had peeled the apple peel off the bottom of Miss Hipbone's shoe. Jilly Cheeter, the girl who'd been given the honour of presenting Tawdry Hipbone with a bouquet of roses, dashed across to where the movie actress's hairpiece had landed as she fell. It wasn't quite a wig. Miss Hipbone still had plenty of jet-black hair (real or otherwise) on top of her beautiful head. It was more like it was for making her hair BIGGER. It looked to Jilly Cheeter like either:

> (a) a very small shaggy
>   black dog

or:

> (b) a very well-fed
>   guinea pig.

It turned out to be (a).

As Jilly Cheeter handed it back to Miss Hipbone it licked her fingers. That way she was able to tell the ball-of-fur's front end.

'Thank you,' said the actress and smiled at Jilly with such a perfect set of gnashers that Jilly was almost blinded by the whiteness of them. Miss Hipbone reached up and pushed the doggy hairpiece back in place.

Jilly Cheeter noticed that, close up, Tawdry Hipbone didn't look quite so young and glamorous as she did from a distance. She could see that the movie star was wearing make-up – *lots* of make-up – but you could still see wrinkles underneath.

Sometimes I spend hours and hours and *hours* in the bath thinking important things — and letting the tiny creatures in my beard enjoy splashing about a bit — until long after the water has gone cold. Whenever I do this, I end up with fingertips more wrinkled than the wrinkliest of prunes. Amazingly, Miss Hipbone's face looked a zillion times wrinklier than that. I'm talking WRINKLED.

'Guess how old I am,' whispered the movie star. (Her breath smelled of Hotty Mintettes.)

Jilly was shocked by the question. She's not that good at guessing grown-ups' ages and knows how important it is not to get it wrong. She reckoned that, from where she was now standing, Tawdry Hipbone looked really old, like FORTY or something, so — to be on the polite side of safe — she said, 'Twenty-eight, Miss Hipbone?'

Miss Hipbone gave a cackling laugh which sounded like someone crinkling up tracing paper. 'Sixty-three!' she said. 'The secret's in the diet.'

Jilly Cheeter was so surprised by this piece of news that, for a moment, she forgot that the capital of France is Paris and thought it was an elephant. She didn't know what to say, so it was rather lucky for her that she – along with just about everyone else – was distracted by Constable Gelatine's nephew, Mustard Tripwire, making an arrest.

The arrestee – or whatever you call the person being arrested – was none other than Bunty Fox.

'What are you charging me with?' she demanded as she struggled to free herself from the young police officer.

'Sniggering at the misfortune of an internationally famous and much-loved film actress!' said Officer Tripwire, even impressing himself.

Everyone cheered. We're not big fans of

Bunty Fox and her family here in Grubtown. They've caused more than their fair share of trouble over the years (and weren't that long out of prison). And nobody likes to see someone with an unfair share of anything, whether it's:

slices of melon

free concert tickets

pancakes

or causing trouble.

At the back of the crowd of onlookers stood a small girl called Emily Blotch. She was standing on a crate of custard pies, labelled: **NOT TO BE USED FOR COMIC EFFECT**, which, I'm pleased to report, they weren't. (Not one of them was thrown during the making of this book.)

Emily is the daughter of Condo Blotch. Nowadays, of course, Condo Blotch is very well-known. You're probably familiar with her chain of ***STOP BEING QUITE SO FAT*** keep-fit centres and have seen her face on the front of magazines and on cartons of the

Condo Blotch **STOP BEING QUITE SO FAT** soft drinks range. At the time of these events, though, Condo was a single mum who worked very hard as a cleaner in a number of places in and around Grubtown.

Next to Emily stood Informative Boothe, town know-all. Unlike everyone else, he didn't appear to be the slightest bit interested in what was going on around him. He had his back to **SMOKY'S** and his head was buried in what looked like a map or a list of instructions, or both. He paced up and down and seemed to be looking for something. At one stage he bumped in Flabby Gomez's son, Tundra, who was supposed to be up at the front of the crowd. Tundra Gomez is now the doorboy – which is a young door*man* – at the cinema, which is why he was there in his impressive doorboy's uniform for the Special Charity Gala Performance of *For the Love of Ducks II*. (The charities in question, by the way, were The Society of Unicyclists

With One Flat Tyre Each and one especially set up for Trying To Find A Way Of Going Back In Time And Saving The Dodo From Extinction And That Kind Of Thing.)

Tundra is a very large lad so, although the adult uniform was far too *long* for him and was trailing along the red carpet, it wasn't nearly w-i-d-e enough for him. He could only do up one button (across a less bulgy part of his body). And even that was putting a serious strain on the gold-braided buttonhole. He was busy trying to push his way to the front of the crowd.

While Bunty Fox was being put in the back of the **GRUBTOWN DOG POUND & FLORAL DELIVERIES** van (which the police department was using until their own van was fixed), Miss Hipbone had made it to her microphone. Like many famous film actors, when she speaks without a script she isn't nearly as interesting as she seems on screen.

'Mr Mayor, ladies and gentlemen,' she said,

'it's so lovely, lovely, lovely to be back in the very town where I was born for this special showing of my latest motion picture.' The dog on top of her hair turned round and snuggled back down again, trying to find a comfortable position. 'I have very lovely, lovely memories of this – er – lovely town so I was delighted to be asked to share this very lovely event with you. I also want to take this opportunity to announce to the WORLD that I shall be marrying my second husband for the third time.'

The crowd cheered and people took lots of photos and Grabby Hanson took lots of cameras.

'I thought it was supposed to be her third husband for the second time?' he whispered to Flabby Gomez.

The mayor wasn't listening. He'd just seen a STRANGE SIGHT at the back of the crowd.

Chapter Two
Gulp!

Jilly Cheeter's best friend Mango Claptrap was really pleased that Jilly had been given the job of handing Tawdry Hipbone the bunch of roses, but he also wished that he'd been given something to do. Actually, he HAD been given something to do but that something-to-do was to be on litter patrol. And litter patrol wasn't quite the something-to-do he'd been hoping to have been given.

Being on litter patrol didn't only mean picking up any litter dropped amongst the feet of the crowd outside **SMOKY'S**. It also meant telling off any people seen dropping litter and warning anyone who appeared to be ABOUT to drop litter *not* to drop it.

So that fellow Grubtowners didn't just think that he was someone being bossy and not minding his own business, Mango Claptrap was given a special cap. Across the front of the special cap, just above the peak, were the words: **ITTER ATROL**. It was an old hat, and the '**L**' and the '**P**' had worn away yonks ago.

'You really should pick up that lolly stick, Mr Scorn,' Mango Claptrap told Acrid Scorn, who'd just tossed it on the pavement.

Mango is a little bit frightened of Acrid Scorn, whose clothes are always full of holes and often smoking slightly from the dangerous chemicals he regularly spills on them.

'What's it to you?' demanded Scorn.

Mango Claptrap pointed to his hat.

'ITTER ATROL? What's that supposed to

mean?' demanded Scorn. 'That's not your name. I know you, Claptrap.'

Mango found himself wishing again that he'd been given another duty. 'Litter Patrol, Mr Scorn. Mayor's orders. Please pick up the lolly stick.'

Acrid Scorn smiled like an evil scarecrow. (There are lots of those about nowadays. Just look out of the nearest window. See?) His job is to dump Grubtown's hazardous waste anywhere but in Grubtown (which isn't a rule he always followed, as readers of *Stinking Rich and Just Plain Stinky* may remember). Here was a man who has pumped gallons of killer-gunk into hollow trees, has filled the forty-foot novelty chipmunk outside '**GNAWING-ANIMALS WORLD**' (*'Where the "Gee!" is Silent.'*) with used-up batteries, and has 'hidden' tonnes of animal manure – poo – under the carpet in the village hall of nearby Werty. And here was a boy wearing *very-silly very-short shorts* fussing over his having dropped a lolly stick.

Acrid Scorn bent down to pick up the stick with a dramatic wave of the arms. 'Well, if it's what the *mayor* wants –' he began, in a put-on whiny voice. Then he stopped.

A large pelican had landed on his bottom, which was sticking skyward as he bent over. Even though the pelican is Grubtown's official town symbol – appearing on everything from the town shield to the mayor's seal (and underwear)

– we'd only had one real-live pelican in town for as long as I could remember. That one pelican's name is Jip and he's the town mascot …but this wasn't Jip, and it was pecking at Acrid Scorn's belt with its huge beak. (It sounded like someone trying to knit with wooden spoons: a sort of *clackerty-click* or *clickerty-clack*.)

And this was what Flabby Gomez had looked across to see at the back of the crowd: an unfamiliar pelican perched on a familiar bottom.

If it had ended there, then the front pages of Grubtown's local newspapers★ would have been very different to how they actually ended up. You see, having very quickly got bored of Scorn's bottom, the Pelican took off and headed straight for Flabby.

Flabby swatted the awkward bird off course, causing it to fly straight into Tawdry Hipbone in a tangle of feathers and beak. Before anyone – including the doggy hairpiece – realised quite

★ *The Grubtown Daily Herald* and
The Grubtown Weekly Gerald

what was happening, the out-of-town bird was flying off with the tiny dog in its great big pedal-bin of a beak!

Officer Tripwire took his gun from the holster on his belt and began shooting at them. Fortunately for the pelican and the dog:

1. Mustard Tripwire is a terrible shot.
2. His gun is a spud-gun. It can only fire bits of potato.

Tripwire's uncle, Constable Gelatine, gave him a clip round the ear. 'What do you think you're doing, you idiot?' he demanded. 'The idea is to RESCUE the dog, not to kill it.'

'Sorry, Uncle,' said Mustard, sheepishly returning the gun to its holster. 'I felt it was important to DO something.'

'**SNOOKS**!' screamed Tawdry Hipbone.

I think a lot of people in the crowd thought she was sneezing; allergic to pelican feathers or something. (That's certainly what *I* thought, and I was sitting quite close to her. Because I'm so important, I got a front-row seat.) The word '**SNOOKS**!' has a real sneezing quality to it, especially the way Miss Hipbone said it.

Then she added: 'My *darling* **SNOOKS**!' so all but the slowest of us – naming no names, Formal Dripping – realised that she must be talking about that extraordinarily fluffy little dog of hers that had just been snatched from the top of her head.

'Do something, Grabby!' shouted the mayor.

Chief Hanson was already punching Garlic Hamper's number into his mobile phone.

The lighthouse keeper answered on the second ring. 'Yup?' he said in such a way that Grabby Hanson could tell he had his pipe clenched between his teeth.

'A pelican with a dog in its beak is currently flying – er – north-north-west from the cinema. See if you can keep it in your sights, will you, Garlic?' said Hanson.

'Will do, Chief,' said Garlic Hamper. He was already grabbing his favourite binoculars and heading for the stairs up to the lantern room where he'd get the best view over Grubtown and, hopefully, of the pelican.

In all the excitement, Jilly Cheeter and Mango Claptrap found themselves side-by-side as best friends often do.

'Did you see that?' gasped Jilly. 'I was right next to Miss Hipbone when Jip grabbed her dog.'

'It wasn't Jip,' said Mango Claptrap excitedly. 'I was right up close to it when it landed on Acrid Scorn's bottom and I could see its markings.'

'A different pelican, huh?' said Jilly Cheeter.

Mango Claptrap nodded. 'What was a dog doing on Tawdry Hipbone's head in the first place?' he asked, which was a good question.

'Good question,' said Jilly Cheeter. 'Perhaps most movie stars keep pets in their hair.' She has a point of course. Cary Grant, Paul Newman, Marilyn Monroe, Johnny Depp, Angelina Jolie and the entire cast of *High School Musicals 1, 2* and *3* all went through a phase of wearing dogs on their heads, didn't they?

They didn't?

I must have been dreaming. I beg your pardon.

'Beardy Ardagh had a salamander in his beard once,' said Mango Claptrap.

'He's not a movie star,' said Jilly.

'And the salamander wasn't a pet,' said

Mango. 'Shall we get an ice-cream?'

'Good idea,' said Jilly Cheeter. And it was.

With everyone running around wondering what to do next, there was no queue for the ice-cream van. Mango took off his **ITTER ATROL** hat and stuffed it in a pocket of his very short shorts. He wouldn't be needing it again that day.

Chapter Three
Whatever she wants

There are four proper hotels in Grubtown and Tawdry Hipbone was staying in all of them. Not all at once. That would be stupid.

And impossible.

Impossibly stupid, in fact.

What I should say is that she had reservations at all of them and checked into all of them, but only stayed in one at a time. This was to confuse the press. Wherever a showbusiness personality as famous as Miss Hipbone goes, photographers follow. Once, one extra-keen photographer – over in Plunge – actually tried hiding in her luggage. Only it turned out *not* to be her luggage but a suitcase belonging to the man in the turban standing next to her. The photographer ended up being kept in storage for six months.

Now the press photographers couldn't all camp outside her Grubtown hotel with their huge cameras and flashing flashguns, loudly slurping coffee out of cardboard cups and telling rude jokes (and generally keeping her awake all night). . . because they didn't know which one of the four proper hotels she was actually in.

When I say proper hotels, I mean ones where the sheets are changed between guests' visits and there are baths and everything. There are, of course, also plenty of 'bed & breakfast' places as well as guest houses and flop houses. A flop house is a hotel where you may end up having to share your bed with anything from a snoring clown (with comedy big shoes) to a hibernating bear to a family of fleas (which is why flop houses are also sometimes called fleabag hotels).

Grubtown's four proper hotels are: The Grand, The Imperial, The Excalibur and **FETTLE'S**. Probably the most exclusive of these is **FETTLE'S**, where the staff are very rude to everyone except their guests. If you nip in there to ask to use their loo, or what time the next bus to Werty leaves, they look down their noses at you as though you're a very small and insignificant piece of toast, made from cheap white bread with all the goodness taken out.

(Because I am such a famous author, they're not quite so rude to me. They don't look quite so far down their noses, and look at me as though I'm only slightly unwelcome.)

The general manager of **FETTLE'S** is Glowering Silt. He is always very smartly dressed, with a fresh yellow rose in the buttonhole of his green pinstripe suit.

It was to **FETTLE'S** that Miss Tawdry Hipbone fled when her Snooks was snatched by that big bird.

'I heard the terrible news,' said Glowering Silt rushing forward. 'Please, come this way.' He led the movie star into his plush, plush offices. In fact, the only plusher rooms in the whole hotel were in the Pelican Suite on the top floor (with its own private lift), where Miss Hipbone would be sleeping that night. (The general manager was hoping beyond hope that Miss Hipbone wouldn't be put off by the fact that the suite was named after the very type of bird which

had made off with her beloved pooch.)

The movie star threw herself into a chair so comfortable that it was like sitting on a giant marshmallow. 'Mr Guilt!' she moaned.

'Silt,' Silt politely reminded her. (It was his being fussy about people getting his name right that made him quit as manager of a very famous hotel in New Amsterdam . . . and how he ended up here in Grubtown.)

'What am I to do? Of course, I cannot leave Grubtown until my poor, sweet Snooks is found.'

'I quite understand,' said Glowering Silt, thinking of all the extra money he'd be making if Tawdry Hipbone stayed longer. The Pelican Suite is a very expensive set of rooms to stay in. 'If there's any way we here at **FETTLE'S** can help you . . .'

'Thank you, Mr Tilt.'

'In the meantime, Miss Hipbone, I shall have the duty manager, Miss Folklore, show you to your room . . . and my name is *Silt*.'

If you're in showbusiness and as famous as Miss Hipbone, people think that you can't do anything on your own, such as tie your shoelaces, throw a stone at a noisy owl or, say, dab perfume on your wrists. You always have someone do it for you. Over time, of course, this means that you really *can't* do anything – cross the road, buy an African daisy, shave a mongoose – without someone actually doing it for you. You've either never learnt or forgotten how. There was NO WAY that Tawdry Hipbone could be expected to make it to the private lift and, from there, to the top floor of **FETTLE'S** and be able to find the Pelican Suite when she got there, even though the only door on the top floor is to the Pelican Suite and there is a brass plaque screwed to it, which reads:

$$\boxed{\text{THE PELICAN SUITE}}$$

Miss Avid Folklore appeared as if by magic. 'If you'd like to come this way, Miss Hipbone,' she said.

'The little girl!' said the movie star.

'The little girl?' asked Glowering Silt and Avid Folklore at EXACTLY the same time.

'When I slipped on an apple peel, a little girl retrieved Snooks for me before that *BEASTLY* bird snatched him away from me! I want you to find her for me and have her brought here! She was so kind ... and it was obvious that Snooks took an instant liking to her.' She wiped away a tear. 'He's such a good judge of character.'

'That would be our pleasure,' said Mr Silt, already calculating the additional costs to add to her bill. 'Consider it done.'

After Jilly Cheeter and Mango Claptrap had finished their ice-creams, they were trying to think how they would go about finding the missing dog.

'Even if we find the pelican, it doesn't necessarily mean we'd find the dog,' said Mango Claptrap.

'No,' agreed Jilly Cheeter. 'It might have eaten it.'

'Or dropped it,' said Mango.

'Or left it in its nest,' said Jilly.

'If only it couldn't fly,' said Mango. 'That would make things a whole lot easier.'

Jilly nodded. 'That way we could have used Harvey. He'd have helped us sniff out the pelican's trail.'

Harvey is the Cheeters' dog. Jilly doesn't have a mum or any brothers or sisters but lives with her dad and Harvey. Harvey is really supposed to be Jilly's dog, but he spends most of his time with Sloop Cheeter, her dad. Jilly was right: Harvey is good at following trails with his nose.

'We could still give it a go,' said Mango Claptrap with excitement. 'If the pelican landed not far away, Harvey might be able to pick up the trail again and lead us to it!'

'But we'd need to give him something with the pelican's scent on it to sniff first,' Jilly Cheeter reminded him.

'I saw the bird land on Acrid Scorn's trousers when he was bending over!' said Mango Claptrap. 'If we could get Harvey to give them a good sniff he might get a good whiff of the pelican!'

'Then we'd better get Harvey and find Acrid Scorn before he changes his trousers.'

'I don't think he *ever* changes his trousers!' said Mango, which wasn't a nice thought.

Chapter Four
On the trail

Chief Grabby Hanson was not having the best of times. He was usually very good at catching people who'd taken things in Grubtown because he's usually the one who's done the taking. But he'd never experienced a pelican snatching a film star's dog before, so he wasn't sure what to do. That didn't stop him taking speedy action, though. Instructing Garlic Hamper to keep a lookout from the top of the lighthouse had been a good move, and he'd also called up the coastguard.

The coastguard station over at Limp has just one helicopter which, for some weird reason, they always call 'the whirligig' (which, according to local know-all Informative Boothe, is also the name of a type of old-fashioned dance). They haven't been able to afford any new parts for the helicopter for years, so they're always having to patch it up, but it still stays up in the air most of the time. What puts some people off is that the windscreen – a sort of plastic bubble taking up much of the front of the thing – is covered in bits of sticking plaster to hide or hold together various chips and cracks.

The coastguard couldn't spare anyone to fly the thing for Grabby Hanson, so Constable Gelatine drove him over to Limp and the chief flew it back, with Gelatine strapped in next to him.

'Keep on the lookout at all times!' Grabby Hanson shouted above the noise of the engine.

'Will do, Chief,' replied his sergeant, looking

through a pair of very powerful binoculars. They were so powerful, in fact, that when Gelatine accidentally looked through them at Grabby Hanson sitting next to him, he could see *so* far up his boss's nose that he was sure he caught a glimpse of his brain.

They headed for Grubtown as fast as the helicopter would take them and only nearly fell out of the sky once. This was the nasty moment when the rotor blades above their heads stopped their whirling for second or two then – after a sound like an otter choking on a piece of tree bark – whizzed back into life. Quite understandably, Gelatine had been terrified. Grabby Hanson, on the other hand, simply carried on looking so cool and calm that even the coolest of cool cucumbers would have been jealous.

The two policemen searched the sky. They swooped over treetops and rooftops. They followed the coast. They followed the river.

They followed the yellowbrick road (or would have done, if Grubtown had one). They tried to think of anywhere a pelican new in town might take a stolen dog.

They came up with zilch.

Absolute zero.

The big nada.

Zip.

Nowt.

Nought.

NOTHING.

They drew a b-l-a-n-k.

Imagine it:

Like that, only, much, much BIGGER. (And I drew that blank myself, by the way. It wasn't done by Jim, the illustrator.)

Finally, as the last drop of fuel evaporated, Chief Grabby Hanson landed the helicopter with a deafening **PLURFFF!** in the field with the giant pencil sharpener (left over from the WORLD BEATERS' FESTIVAL).

He hopped out of the cockpit as if he'd just been for a gentle spin in an old sports car. 'Come on, Gelatine,' he said. 'You get hold of Luminous Shard to get this thing up and running again, and I'll carry on the search.' He strode off through the tangled grass, speaking into his police radio.

Luminous Shard, in case you've forgotten – and are TOO LAZY to look in the list at the back of the book – is a mechanic (and the second-most bald person in Grubtown). The MOST bald person is Manual Org, who doesn't have a single hair anywhere on his body, which makes him BALD CHAMPION.

Constable Gelatine unclipped his radio from his belt and called his nephew. 'Are you there, Mustard?' he asked.

'Reading you loud and clear, Uncle,' said Officer Mustard Tripwire. *'Have you found Miss Hipbone's dog?'*

''Fraid not,' said Gelatine. 'No sign of it or the pelican. What have you done with Bunty Fox?'

'Made her fill in a pile of time-wasting forms till she got wrist ache, then I let her off with a stern warning.'

'You're learning well, Mustard,' said Constable Gelatine, the pride showing in his voice.

'Thanks,' said Tripwire. '*I've learnt from the best.*'

'Out of interest,' said Gelatine, 'what forms did you have her fill?'

'*The one we give people who are applying not to have to wear a hat on Grubtown's Gotta Getta Hat Day. One which my vet gave me to fill out before getting worming tablets for my new rabbit, and an application form for permission to carry live snakes in an open-top vehicle,*' Mustard Tripwire explained. '*Not that Mrs Fox knew that, Uncle.*'

'Sergeant,' Gelatine reminded him. 'Good work, lad.'

Harvey is quite a big dog with very floppy ears, a very friendly expression and a very licky, lolling tongue. He's the kind of dog who tries SO hard to do as he's told but finds it difficult because everything around him is so interesting.

Snuffle.

Snuffle.

Sniff.

Tail-wag.

Tail-wag.

Jilly had found Harvey curled up at her dad's feet whilst he was doing one of his word-search comics. Her dad had been outside the cinema to watch Jilly present the flowers to Tawdry Hipbone but when things had got a bit crazy had decided to go back home.

Harvey was pulling Jilly along with his bright red lead, sniffing the ground this way and that, hoovering up heaven-knows-what with his mouth every now and then.

'Now all we need to do is to find Acrid Scorn,' said Mango Claptrap. 'Then Harvey can get a sniff of that pelican from the bottom of his trousers, and we're off!'

Like many a Grubtowner, Acrid Scorn could often be found drinking a mug of something at THE RUSTY DOLFPHIN overlooking the beach, but not that day. This was because the cafe still hadn't been rebuilt following an accident involving a ship.

Jilly suggested that they go and see Acrid's brother, Lefty Scorn, at Scorn's, Grubtown's laundrette and jewellery shop. 'He might know where he is,' she said.

Inside the shop they found Lefty Scorn helping Mrs Awning out of one of the huge hot-air clothes dryers which she'd somehow managed to fall into whilst trying to retrieve a sock (which wasn't even hers).

Jilly Cheeter and Mango Claptrap waited patiently by a display of watchstraps which smelt like the inside of an expensive car. They'd left Harvey outside, his lead tied to a lamppost.

When Mr Scorn had managed to steer – the very hot – Mrs Awning out of the shop and into a taxi to take her home, he turned his attention to the children. 'And what can I do for you two?' he asked.

'We're looking for your brother, Mr Scorn,' said Mango Claptrap.

'What's he done this time?' asked Lefty Scorn with a sigh.

'Nothing,' said Jilly.

'The pelican that stole Tawdry Hipbone's dog perched on his bottom first,' Mango Claptrap explained.

'And that somehow makes the whole thing Acrid's fault?'

'No, not at all –' began Mango.

'You see, Mr Scorn,' Jilly interrupted, 'we thought that if Harvey –'

'Her dog,' said Mango.

'– my dog,' said Jilly, 'could get a good scent of the pelican off the bottom of your brother's trousers, we might be able to track the bird down.'

'And possibly find the missing dog?' asked Lefty Scorn.

'Yes!' said Jilly Cheeter.

'Precisely!' said Mango Claptrap.

'It might be worth a try,' agreed the jeweller-cum-laundryman, 'but I'm not sure how Acrid might feel about it.'

'We were thinking of getting Harvey to give the bottom of your brother's trousers a good sniff *without him realising what we're doing*,' Jilly confessed.

Lefty Scorn's face broke into a grin. He could just imagine the scene. 'Now *that*,' he beamed, 'is a good plan!'

Chapter Five
On yer bike

Hobo Browne is a homeless person, a tramp, a gentleman of the road, a scruffy layabout, a man fallen on hard times, a happy-go-lucky chappy, a bearded bloke, or all or none of these things. It depends who you talk to. But one thing's as sure as my name is Beardy: that when that pelican stole Tawdry Hipbone's little dog Snooks, he was one of three temporary part-time washer-uppers in the kitchens deep in the depths of FETTLE'S.

On the day of the dognap, however, he was told to hang up his apron, rubber gloves and brush and go in search of Jilly Cheeter to whom Snooks and Miss Hipbone had apparently taken an instant liking. They offered him double pay and lent him Avid Folklore's bicycle. It was a very nice one. It was very shiny with a big bell and even had a little saddlebag at the back.

The truth be told, Hobo Browne has no idea how to ride a bike but didn't want to hurt

anybody's feelings, so wheeled it round the corner out of sight, and then threw it into the hotel pond, where it promptly sank without trace in the dark green water. That way, he reasoned, it would be assumed that he was riding it, and everyone would be happy.

He then set off on foot whistling '**If I Had To Eat You I Wish You Were Soup**', a song he's heard the Grumbly girls sing far

more often than he cares to remember. It's one of those songs no one particularly likes, but everyone somehow ends up humming, or whistling, or singing, or playing, or tapping on to the head of the bald lady sitting in front of them on the bus, using a plastic ruler.

What's always bothered me about the song is that you don't eat soup. You drink it – it's not a knife-and-fork meal but needs the spoon or mug approach – so either the song should be called 'If I Had To *Drink* You I Wish You Were Soup' or, for example, 'If I Had To Eat You I Wish You Were *Stew*'.

I doubt any of these kinds of thought were going through Hobo's mind as he made his way from **FETTLE'S** into town. He knew full-well where Jilly Cheeter lived, but he hadn't told Mr Silt that. He wanted to take his time finding Jilly. He was being paid by the hour and just about anything beat washing up in that windowless hot kitchen except for the following jobs Hobo

Browne has done – a few days here, a few days there – in the past:

★ cleaning out the insides of the CENSORED

↰ Don't ask!

★ gathering up all the cowpats from Wretching's Dairy by hand

★ Swimming in a pool of m—

Come to think of it, this is making me a bit queasy, so I think I'll stop if you don't mind. Simply imagine Hobo Browne whistling the Grumbly girls' soup song as he headed into town.

He decided that it might be nice to walk down Flimsy Road and across (the new) Flimsy Bridge. Only an IDIOT would try driving across Flimsy Bridge – even the new one – and Formal Dripping doesn't have a car.

Walking down Flimsy Road meant passing

Manual Org's place. Manual Org's place isn't a house but a tree. Mr Org is Grubtown's very richest citizen but he chooses to live in a tree because he wants to. And it's no ordinary tree: it's covered in more baubles than the most showy-offy Christmas tree, and these are all REAL DIAMONDS!!! (No one except Chief Grabby Hanson has ever stolen any, and he's always put them back.) Everyone loves Manual Org.

I love Manual Org. The Mayor, Flabby Gomez, loves Manual Org. Jilly Cheeter loves Manual Org. Mango Claptrap loves Manual Org. Jilly Cheeter's dad, Sloop Cheeter, loves Manual Org. Mango Claptrap's mum –

Hey! I've got an idea. Why not read all the names in the list of townsfolk at the back of the book and say the words 'loves Manual Org' after each of them? It doesn't have to be out loud.

'Hi, Hobo!' said Manual Org as the gentleman of the road came in to view.

'Hello, Mr Org!' said Hobo Browne. 'A beautiful evening.'

'They all are,' said Informative Boothe suddenly appearing from behind a bush at the roadside, giving Hobo Browne quite a shock. Informative Boothe was studying that selfsame half-map-half-instructions he'd been so interested in when pacing up and down outside the cinema.

Hobo Browne came to an abrupt halt and gave serious consideration to Informative Boothe's comment that all evenings are beautiful. 'Do you know what, Mr

Boothe?' he said. 'I think you're right.'

Grubtown's resident know-all nodded. 'I usually am,' he agreed, without looking up from the map.

'Treasure hunt?' Manual Org asked him, peering over his shoulder at the map.

'Of sorts,' Informative Boothe replied. 'Good day to you both.'

'Bye,' said Org, turning his attention back to Hobo Browne. 'Heading anywhere in particular?' he asked.

'I'm cycling in search of Jilly Cheeter,' said the tramp.

'But without a bike?' said Manual Org.

'See what you mean,' Hobo Browne mumbled into his wild grey beard. 'Dunno how to ride. Never have.'

'Cup of slerch?' Manual Org offered.

'Don't mind if I do,' said Hobo Browne with a happy grin. He watched Informative Boothe disappear around a bend in the road, his nose still in the map.

We drink a lot of slerch in Grubtown. Tea and coffee are both popular – especially in tea shops and coffee shops – but when we Grubtowners are at home, slerch is probably the hot beverage of choice.

It was whilst Manual Org and Hobo Browne were enjoying their second mug of slerch – with just a dash of periwinkle – that who should walk under the branch they were sitting on but Jilly Cheeter and Mango Claptrap, two of Manual Org's favourite people. (If you want to know why, perhaps you could check out some back issues of our local papers.★)

They all greeted each other. Harvey the dog jumped up and did some slobbery licks which are doggy equivalents of everything from a casual 'Hi, how are you?' to a kiss.

'I've been sent to find you, Miss Cheeter,' said Hobo (whose teeth are even more crooked and yellow than mine).

★ *The Grubtown Daily Herald* and
The Grubtown Weekly Gerald

'Who by?' asked Jilly.

'The general manager at Fettle's.'

'Fettle's?' asked Jilly.

'The swankiest hotel in town!' said Mango Claptrap, who tends to know stuff like that.

Hobo Browne nodded. 'That film actress is staying on the whole top floor and she wants to see you. I'm to bring you back and to take you to Miss Folklore, the duty manager, who will take you to Mr Silt, the general manager, who will take you to Miss What's-Her-Name.'

'Tawdry Hipbone,' said Mango Claptrap. 'I wonder what she wants with you, Jilly?'

'Why not come with me and find out,' said Jilly Cheeter. 'We can always do the trouser-sniffing thing another time.'

'Trouser-sniffing?' asked a slightly puzzled Manual Org. I'm sure he would have raised an eyebrow if he had one. (He doesn't have a single hair on his body, remember. Not even up his nose.)

'Not *our* trousers,' Mango Claptrap explained, (which was a pretty silly thing to say because Jilly was wearing that nice dress she always does and he was wearing his weird short shorts).

'*Acrid Scorn*'s trousers,' added Jilly Cheeter, as though that would somehow make things clearer.

'And Harvey here will do the sniffing,' Mango explained.

'I'm not sure Mr Silt will like you bringing a dog into Fettle's,' said Hobo Browne a little uncertainly.

'He won't mind,' said Manual Org. 'If I know posh hotel managers, he'll do anything to please a rich and famous guest, and we know that a certain Miss Hipbone LOVES dogs!'

'Okay, then,' said Hobo Browne. 'Let's go, but not too quickly, if you don't mind, please. I'm not in a hurry to get back to those stacks of dirty dishes.'

And off they went, leaving Manual Org

wiping out his empty mugs with a large dock leaf.

Jilly and Mango had done their best to find Acrid Scorn but he'd been nowhere to be found. It later turned out that this was because he was busy illegally pumping toxic waste into a lake just outside the town's limits. When members of the Fox family found out they were DELIGHTED. To them a lake only means one thing: A PLACE FOR DUCKS TO LIVE AND PLAY AND TO LAY EGGS TO MAKE *MORE* DUCKS. But now the lake was ruined!

Hobo Browne arrived back at **FETTLE'S** with Jilly Cheeter, Mango Claptrap and Harvey.

Miss Avid Folklore had obviously been on the lookout for them because she came out of the building to greet them on the gravel.

'Excellent work, Hobo,' she said, looking around, 'but what did you do with my bicycle? I realised I left all my keep-me-alive pills in the saddlebag and I need them like – er – *now*.'

Hobo Browne didn't have an answer for that. He hadn't been thinking that far ahead.

Chapter Six
Stuff happens

Whilst Miss Folklore was being taken away in the ambulance, Dr Fraud at her side, Jilly Cheeter and Mango Claptrap were taken to Mr Silt's office suite.

'Come!' said a voice. Glowering Silt would make a good old-fashioned headmaster. One of those ones who thinks there's still a war on. Jilly and Mango went inside. 'Welcome, children,' said Silt with what he hoped was a friendly smile. Like most sensible adults, the general manager of **FETTLE'S** doesn't like children. But he does like making his guests happy, particularly when that guest is as famous and as RICH as Miss Tawdry Hipbone is. 'Peppermint?' he asked.

On his desk was what looked like a silver ball on a three-legged stand but he'd rolled the top back to reveal a nest of peppermints.

'No, thank you,' said Jilly Cheeter politely.

Mango Claptrap was already filling the pockets of his shorts. '*Thanksh,*' he said through stuffed cheeks.

The manager eyed Mango with interest. 'You're Mango Claptrap, aren't you?' he asked.

'*Yesch,*' said Mango, a peppermint ball shooting out of his mouth and across the room.

'How nice to have the both of you here,' he said.

Mango Claptrap and Jilly Cheeter are well-known in and around Grubtown. There's a humongous diamond named after them in the town museum, and they've been awarded medals by Mayor Flabby Gomez on more than one occasion.

'Miss Hipbone has asked to see you in person, Miss Cheeter,' said the manager. 'Would you please follow me? You too, Master Claptrap, if you like.'

'I like.' Mango Claptrap nodded.

All three of them walked out of the office, across the marble floor of the foyer, into the penthouse lift and up to the top floor.

Glowering Silt knocked on the door to Tawdry Hipbone's rooms whilst Jilly Cheeter looked at her reflection in the plaque:

THE PELICAN SUITE

She could see that she had a smudge of something on her cheek and was busy trying to rub it off with a wet thumb when the door flew open.

Tawdry Hipbone stood framed in the doorway, every inch (and centimetre) a film star. She was wearing a potato sack.

No, seriously. Years ago, a famous film critic wrote that Miss Hipbone would look good dressed in *anything*. Six months later, a calendar appeared with a photograph of her wearing a different crazy thing for each month, from a barrel with braces in January to some very large leaves in December. She'd found October – the potato sack – really comfortable to wear and would often slip into it (or a similar sack) when she was relaxing on her own.

'You found her, Mr Spilt!' said the movie star with delight, her eyes flitting from Jilly Cheeter to Glowering Silt then back again.

'Nothing is too much trouble at Fettle's,' said the manager. He made a slight bow, then turned and left. He didn't even mention that his name was actually 'Silt'. He was thinking how much '**MISSION ACCOMPLISHED**' stamped on her bill would add to the cost of her stay.

'Come in! Come in!' said Tawdry Hipbone ushering the two children into her hotel suite.

Neither Jilly nor Mango had ever seen anything like it. It was bigger than both their houses. Maybe not both their houses put together, but certainly bigger than each house on its own. And, unlike both of their houses, the suite was beautifully decorated and full of stylish furniture.

'This place is like a palace!' Mango Claptrap gawked.

'It *is* pretty amazing!' agreed Jilly Cheeter.

'I'd swap it for a prison cell if it meant my getting my little Snooks back!' said Tawdry Hipbone with a dramatic sigh. She slumped into a chair the size of something far too big to be called that.

'This is my best friend, Mango Claptrap,' said Jilly Cheeter. 'Why did you want to see me, Miss Hipbone?'

'Because you were so kind,' said the film star. 'Because I could see that Snooks liked you the moment you picked him up. I sense that you understand *him* and you understand my pain. I feel sure —'

'We've been trying to find a way of tracking your dog down,' said Mango excitedly.

'See!' said Hipbone with obvious delight. 'I just KNEW you'd care!'

'I have a dog, a big shaggy one called Harvey,'

said Jilly and she went on to explain about their idea of trying to get him to pick up the scent of the strange pelican off Acrid Scorn's trousers.

Tawdry Hipbone whooped with delight.

'WHOOP!' she said.

With delight.

'You kids are amazing!'

Harvey had been tied up outside the hotel. Within ten minutes, he was up in the suite with them, chewing on a bone with a spare bone waiting for him on a very expensive dinner plate. They were making plans.

The people. Not the bones.

Chapter Seven
Taking action

Mayor Flabby Gomez was having a bad day. It should have been a good day. This was the day where he got to share a platform with a world-famous movie actress. The day where he got to make a speech (and Flabby LOVES making speeches). The day where he would be one of the first people to see *For the Love of Ducks II* . . .

. . . only it hadn't happened that way, of course. And what *had* happened instead? A complete and utter disaster.

When that out-of-town pelican had flown straight at him, what had he done? Flabby Gomez had gone over the events again and again in his mind. Every time it came out the same. He had batted the bird aside with his hands, SENDING IT STRAIGHT INTO MISS HIPBONE'S HAIR.

If only he'd been sensible enough and polite enough to knock the pelican in the *other* direction.

It might well have simply flown away.

But, *no*. He went and drove it straight on a collision course with a mega-famous movie queen and the stupid bird had gone and stolen Miss Hipbone's precious pooch!

Miss Hipbone was probably the most famous person to come out of Grubtown after Hybrid Byword and Purple Outing! And, if not *the* richest (Purple Outing and Manual Org beat her when it came to wealth) she was certainly far richer than HE was.

Things could hardly be worse.

To cheer himself up, the mayor decided to fix himself a snack, which (in order of size) comes between 'a lite bite' and 'a snackette'. If you don't believe me, here's the list in full, starting with the biggest:

1st   Total blow-out
2nd   Feast (aka banquet)
3rd   Sheer piggery
4th   Full meal
5th   Light meal (as in 'a little light supper')
6th   Lite bite (aka quick bite)
7th   Snack
8th   Snackette
9th   A little something
10th A nibble
11th A taste
12th A crumb

Having said that, it's important to remember that your idea of a snack and Flabby's idea of a snack could be the difference between chalk and a sandwich so tall that you'd need a ladder to reach the top of it and some head-for-height pills to climb it.

Anyway, what Flabby Gomez needed right at that moment was comfort food and that was exactly what he was having at one end of the table, while Chief of Police Grabby Hanson sat at the other, with Sergeant Constable Gelatine on the chief's left and Mustard

Tripwire on his right.

'How am I ever going to get elected mayor again if we can't find this missing dog?' said Flabby, between mouthfuls.

'That's easy, Mr Mayor,' said Grabby. 'You're the only one with a vote around here, and you're hardly likely to vote for someone else . . .'

'That's not the point, Chief,' said Flabby Gomez. 'I won't be able to hold my head up high.'

'You weren't responsible for Snooks's safety,' said Grabby Hanson. 'I'm the chief of police around here, remember, Mr Mayor. Security is MY responsibility.'

'And I was the one who fired my potato gun at it and –' began Officer Mustard Tripwire.

Constable Gelatine shook his head at his nephew across the table, and Tripwire became silent. He looked down at his hands. They were supposed to leave the talking to Hanson. This was official town business and official Grubtown business is handled in a particular way.

Mayor Flabby Gomez kept his eyes on Grabby Hanson's handsome features as he finished a mouthful of sliced dill pickles.

'Any suggestions?'

'I'm working on three possibilities at the moment, Mr Mayor,' said Grabby Hanson. 'One, that Snooks and the pelican are still together. Two, that the pelican dropped Snooks from a great height – SPLAT! – and that Snooks is now in doggy heaven, with a little doggy harp and a pair of little doggy wings –'

Flabby Gomez groaned and covered his eyes with a mayonnaise-smeared hand. 'And Three?' he asked.

'That the pelican either dropped Snooks near enough the ground for the dog to be unharmed, or landed somewhere and Snooks climbed out of its beak.'

Gomez licked his fingers.

'For the time being, I'm going to rule out One, because I can't imagine a pelican flying around all this time with a dog in its beak,' Grabby Hanson continued. 'I'm going to rule out Two because, for the purposes of this investigation, we HAVE to assume that Snooks is alive, so we need to concentrate on Three.'

'That the pelican has played its part and we're now looking for a dog on its own, which could have been dropped anywhere?' said Flabby Gomez.

'Exactly, Mr Mayor. A simple missing dog

case . . . except that the dog could be anywhere and Tawdry Hipbone is Tawdry Hipbone.'

'What about the world's press?' asked Flabby Gomez.

'We're very fortunate that most of them couldn't find Grubtown in time to witness the – er – unfortunate events outside Smoky's cinema . . . and, even if the news has since leaked out, most of them are stuck on that broken-down train a few miles outside Fugg Station or are being held up by the roadworks out on Big Road.'

The mayor raised an eyebrow like a question mark. It was the first he'd heard of a broken-down train and any roadworks.

'Constable?' said the chief of police.

'My sister Galaxy – young Mustard here's mother – drives the train between here and Werty during the week, Mr Mayor. I gave her a call and suggested that her engine might have engine trouble. She chose to stop in the most middle-of-nowhere place she could think of on the line.'

Flabby grinned. (There was a piece of spinach between his teeth.) This was the first good news he'd heard in hours. 'Good work, Gelatine!'

'Thank you, sir.'

'And the roadworks?'

'I had a word with Rambo Sanskrit,' said Grabby Hanson. 'He had half the council workers digging up all six lanes of Big Road before you could say free ice-creams for everyone!'

'And what about the photographers already here in town for the film premiere?' asked Flabby Gomez.

'By an extraordinary coincidence, they're surrounded by a herd of escaped cows from Wretching's Dairy ... I accidentally left the gate

to their field open myself,' said Chief Hanson. 'It was very careless of me.'

Mayor Flabby Gomez got to his feet. 'Gentlemen,' he said, with a most solemn expression. 'You are the finest police force in the world.' Then he handed round some cheese and biscuits.

Chapter Eight
A right Pasting

Jilly Cheeter had a bright idea. It came from remembering one of Tawdry Hipbone's old films. In the weeks leading up to Miss Hipbone's visit, **SMOKY'S** had been showing a Tawdry Hipbone 'retrospective' which is just a big word for 'bunch of old films'. (Some of these were *so* old that they weren't even in colour but were black and white. It didn't matter much because one was about nuns and the other about penguins and they're mostly black and white even when they're in colour, if you see what I mean.)

'I've had an idea!' said Jilly Cheeter leaping up from the leatherette footstool she'd been using as a chair.

Tawdry Hipbone was standing by one of the many floor-to-ceiling windows in the Pelican Suite, watching a funny little man with his nose in a map wander past way down below. 'An idea about what, dear?' she asked

'About how we can track down Acrid Scorn and his trousers?' Mango Claptrap asked keenly.

'No, *another* way of finding the pelican! You know that film you were in about the oil-drinking monster . . . ?'

'*It Came From Somewhere Over There, I Think*?' said a now VERY excited Mango Claptrap. He'd loved that film. 'The one with the Orgon, a hairy beast from outer space, who was drinking the world's oil supplies and the hero, Captain JoJo, found a way of capturing it by baiting a trap with crude oil –'

'That's it!' said Jilly Cheeter.

'I spent most of my time screaming in that movie,' said Tawdry Hipbone, 'or clinging to the captain's arm ... or screaming *and* clinging to the captain's arm at the same time. It really gave me a chance to show a whole range of feelings.' (Actors often speak about stuff like that.) She had a faraway look in her eyes.

'You think we should bait some kind of trap to catch the pelican?' Mango asked Jilly.

She nodded.

'You're a genius!' said her best friend.

'But what? How?' asked Miss Hipbone.

'Well, because it's a seabird we're after and not a space monster, what if we smeared something with fishpaste?' said Jilly, barely able to contain her excitement. 'Whenever I eat my fishpaste sandwiches on the jetty, it attracts Jip.'

'Jip?'

'The town pelican.'

'I remember him!' said Miss Hipbone with a nod.

'What about Fettle's?' shouted Mango Claptrap, adjusting his short shorts. 'Why not smear the roof of THIS HOTEL with fishpaste? It's a tall building, high enough to be in a visiting pelican's flight path!'

'Brilliant idea, Mango!' said Jilly. Then she suddenly looked less sure. 'But what if Mr Silt minds about his hotel being smeared with fishpaste?'

'*Mind*?' said Miss Hipbone. 'Why should Mr Slip MIND? He's here to serve . . . to look after his guests. I'll pay him handsomely and, if I get my Snooks back, I'll recommend this place to all my famous friends. I wouldn't be surprised if he doesn't spread the first smear of fishpaste on a roof-tile himself.'

She picked up the old-fashioned gold-plated telephone linked directly to Mr Silt's office and spoke into it. 'Mr Wilt? I want your people to lay their hands on as much fishpaste as possible and for you to cover Fettle's roof with it immediately. . . Why? You ask me *why*? Does it really matter, Mr Quilt? Because I'm a guest and I'm asking you to. . . What's that? Why, yes, I'm sure smoked-mackerel pâté would do just as well. Thank you. It needs to be done before nightfall!'

She flashed a film star smile in the direction of Jilly Cheeter and Mango Claptrap. 'You two,' she beamed, 'are a pair of smart cookies!'

Harvey, meanwhile, was more interested in sniffing one of Miss Hipbone's sweaters which she had draped over the arm of a sofa the size of a mini-submarine. (But not *that* mini.)

I must confess that I never thought I'd live to see the day when the staff of **FETTLE'S** – from bellhops to chambermaids to managers – smeared the hotel's higgledy-piggledy roofs with best smoked-mackerel pâté, but see it I did.

Even from down on the ground, we onlookers could catch a whiff of fish every time the breeze blew in the right direction.

No sooner had the first few smears been spread than the seagulls started to arrive and then more and then more and then MORE until it was hard for the hotel staff to spread the rest of the fish pâté over the uncovered tiles.

Next came the ducks, probably interested in seeing what all the fuss was about.

Then came Jip. Jip is an extremely lazy bird and seems to do as little flying as possible. He'd far rather the food came to *him*. Failing that, he waddles short distances or hopes that Mayor Flabby Gomez will carry him around under his arm, which he often does.

This time, though, he really did rise to the occasion. Jip rose up off the ground and came in to land on top of the roof, skidding on a thick blob of pâté. It was one of the most appetising roofs he'd ever smelt!

And then . . . and then – incredibly – another pelican came into view. The *other* pelican. It landed far more gracefully than Jip ever could and seemed more interested in him than any fish food.

Jilly Cheeter's and Mango Claptrap's plan had worked . . . as long as they could catch the pelican, that is.

Each pelican started tapping either side of the other's beak, a bit like a sword fight, but with pelican beaks pointing downwards. It made a very satisfying *clacking* sound. (Once heard, never forgotten.)

'They like each other!' whispered Mango Claptrap to Jill Cheeter. They were crouched in the stairwell of a fire exit which led out onto a flat part of the roof.

'I wonder if that new one is a *lady* pelican,' said Jilly.

'Excuse me,' said Flabby Gomez, who had appeared on the stairs behind them. He looked

puffed out after all that climbing. Grabby Hanson – who was positioned on the roof – had radioed the mayor to tell him that both Jip and the 'target bird **CODENAME: DOGNAPPER**' had gone for the bait and were now on the roof.

Because the mayor has such a good relationship with Jip, it was suggested that he come and try to get close enough to grab Dognapper. Otherwise, they'd have to try using the big nets.

Everyone who'd been spreading the roof now stood still. The seagulls kept on squawking, though, so the pelican didn't seem to notice the change in atmosphere. Flabby somehow managed to squeeze between Jilly and Mango and was now on the roof. He heaved himself over the (very slippery) air-conditioning unit, and made his way towards Jip and Dognapper.

'Hello, boy,' he said. 'Fancy seeing you up here.' He pulled a fishfinger out of his pocket and took a step closer. Mango wasn't sure whether he'd brought a fishfinger with him especially, or whether Flabby always carried one around with him in case he got a little peckish.

Jip turned to look at his friend Flabby, probably pleased that he'd get carried back down rather than having to do that tiring flapping-of-wings thing. Imagine his surprise, then, when Flabby Gomez picked up the OTHER pelican and tucked it under his arm. It didn't seem to mind. It looked quite happy, in fact, and made an I'm-quite-happy sort of sound.

Very carefully, the mayor then managed to pick up Jip with his free hand and to tuck him under the *other* arm. Jilly Cheeter, Mango Claptrap, Chief Hanson, Mr Silt and the assembled company all held their breath as they watched. Flabby Gomez now walked – no, strolled – back inside the building with both birds.

But now what?

This, dear reader, was the BIG hole in Jilly Cheeter and Mango Claptrap's plan. This was the hole **SO LARGE** that you could drive a truck through it with everyone leaning out of the windows waving their arms about – which you should *never* do in a moving vehicle – and you STILL wouldn't touch the sides. Binkey the pelican (as Flabby later named Dognapper) was now safely in the mayor's care, but how did that get them any nearer to finding Snooks? It wasn't as if they could ask the pelican what it had done with the poor dog!

Oh dear.

Oh dear.

Oh *dear*.

Chapter Nine
Not to be sniffed at

Flabby Gomez was with Jip and Binkey in the bathroom of the Pelican Suite, running a bath for them to bob about in, the way pelicans like to. Grabby Hanson was deep in conversation with Glowering Silt in one corner of the sitting room. Tawdry Hipbone was perched on the arm of an armchair so bright red that it couldn't be more red if it wanted to be (even if there were BIG PRIZES on offer).

Jilly Cheeter and Mango Claptrap, meanwhile, were looking for a missing dog.

Not Snooks, but Harvey.

In all the excitement, he had somehow got out of Tawdry's suite and was now nowhere to be found . . . The first place they looked was the hotel's kitchens, but he hadn't been there. Next, they tried outside.

They found Hobo Browne standing in the pond holding a rather nice bicycle (with a saddlebag) covered in weed of pleasing shades of green.

'Hello, Mr Browne!' said Mango.

'Hello, Mango!' said Hobo Browne. He waded back over to the bank. 'Give me a hand, will you?'

'Sure,' said Mango Claptrap, taking the bicycle off him and laying it on the ground.

He and Jilly Cheeter reached out an arm each. Hobo grabbed hold of them and heaved himself out of the water.

'Have you seen Harvey?' asked Jilly.

'Oh, yes,' said Hobo Browne. 'I saw him

heading off that way about twenty minutes ago.' He pointed down the driveway towards town.

'Perhaps he's gone home to your dad?' Mango Claptrap suggested to Jilly. 'He'll find the way. He has a good sense of smell.'

Jilly sniffed the air. It still smelt of smoked mackerel. The last of the pâté had long since disappeared from the hotel roof, but the sky was full of seagulls with fishy breath. '*Everywhere* smells plain fishy to me at the moment,' she said.

It was beginning to get dark when they found Harvey. He was outside Smoky's – sorry, that should be **SMOKY'S** – cinema, sniffing around. He was on the spot where Jilly had picked up Snooks when he'd first fallen out of Miss Hipbone's hair.

'*There* you are,' said Jilly, rubbing him behind the ears when he bounded up to her. 'What are you up to, boy?'

'Woof,' said Harvey, which is just about all he can say out loud (apart from a strange whining noise and some eager panting).

'He probably smelt Snooks's scent on some of Miss Hipbone's clothes,' said Mango, 'then sniffed it again here on his way to your house.'

Suddenly, Harvey was off again, floppy ears bouncing. Readers of earlier **GRuBtoWN taLes** may remember that our cinema is built on the site of the old smoke houses – where Grubtowners used to smoke kippers – at the very top of an impressively hilly hill. (In fact, it's called Impressively Hilly Hill. Or 'the hill' for short.) Jilly Cheeter and Mango Claptrap bounded after him.

By the time they caught up with Harvey, he was on a wide stretch of beach, snuffling along the sand, sneezing at the occasional piece of bleached driftwood or startled starfish.

'Gotcha!' said Jilly grabbing his collar. Harvey was showing real interest in a metal thingummy poking out of the sand. Mango gave it a yank.

'It looks like a crown!' he joked, holding it above his head. Then he looked at it more closely. It really *did* look like a crown, only all dull and brown.

'Look!' said Jilly. She was pointing at a big clump of seaweed, only it wasn't really a big clump of seaweed. It was a medium-sized clump of seaweed and a small hairy dog which looked like a hairpiece. 'It's Snooks! Harvey has found Snooks!'

'Good boy, Harvey!' said Mango and Jilly at the same time.

Just then, a man started running towards them across the sand. As he got closer, Jilly Cheeter recognised him as Informative Boothe, Grubtown's resident know-all. She had never seen him *run* before. She had never seen him this EXCITED before.

'I don't believe it!' he shouted, waving what

looked to Mango and Jilly like an old map.
'You found it!'

'My dog did,' said Jilly proudly, then
she realised that Mr Boothe wasn't talking

about Snooks.

He took the piece of metal from Mango Claptrap's hand, holding it up to the sun. 'You've found the Wormwood Crown!'

★ ★ ★

And so it was that Miss Tawdry Hipbone got her darling Snooks back, recommended **FETTLE'S** (and 'the charming Mr Stilt') to all her superstar friends, and married her third husband for the second time . . . or her second husband for the third time. Miss Avid Folklore recovered from her lack of pills and her bicycle recovered from its short time in the hotel pond.

Having found Binkey, a pelican ladyfriend, Jip now spends most of his time with her. (One year Binkey laid an egg, but it never hatched.) Sometimes Mayor Flabby Gomez takes Jip for an under-arm walk, sometimes Binkey, and sometimes both of them. All three really seem to understand each other.

Talking of Flabby, the mayor presented Constable Gelatine's sister Galaxy Tripwire – she's married to Relish Tripwire, Mustard's dad – with a special certificate for making sure that her train broke down with the world's press on board. And the workmen who dug up Big Road got those ice-creams they were promised. (As for the cows from *Wretching's Dairy*, they were soon rounded up and given extra salt-lick by way of a 'Thank you!'.)

And Jilly Cheeter and Mango Claptrap? They were not only the heroes of the hour – though both of them insisted that Harvey should get most of the credit – but they'd also found the Wormwood Crown. Back in 1817, a postal worker by the name of Careworn Wormwood had declared Grubtown an independent kingdom and himself king. 'King Wormwood' ruled for just seven days (nine if you count the weekend twice), before being dragged from his bed and locked up in a beer cellar over in Limp. His crown was put on display in the town hall, but in 1848 – around about the time that Grabby Hanson's ancestors first settled in the neighbourhood – it mysteriously disappeared . . . until now. It turned out that Informative

Boothe had been on the trail of it for months, having recently discovered 'a part-map and part-list-of-instructions' in the back of a long-forgotten book in the Grubtown Town Council Archives.

Today, the crown is in The Grubtown Museum, alongside the Claptrap-Cheeter Diamond. There was a special unveiling ceremony with a blue curtain and everything. You can read about it in our local papers.★ Miss Tawdry Hipbone flew in specially with Snooks, and Acrid Scorn – who, for some reason, was in charge of cleaning up afterwards – was wearing a new pair of trousers. It wasn't that he wanted to look smart for the occasion. (He didn't care.) It was because the chemical spills on his old pair had finally eaten them away to next-to-nothing. Nowadays this 'new' pair is already covered in holes and blotches and giving off puffs of foul-smelling smoke.

Jilly Cheeter has a photograph of the event

★ *The Grubtown Daily Herald* and
  The Grubtown Weekly Gerald

on her bedroom wall. In front of the glass case containing the crown is Flabby Gomez in his fine blue robe, Chief Grabby Hanson in his best police uniform, Miss Hipbone (dressed in a barrel and braces) and Mango and Jilly herself. Snooks is lying in his mistress's jet-black hair. Leaning down from the top of the case is Jip, with a fish in his mouth. He's trying to feed it to the wrong end of the dog.

THE END

Another word from Beardy Ardagh

For some unexplained reason, some of you weirdos not only like writing to me about **GRuBtoWN taLes** but also appreciate a reply. If you do write, I suggest you address the envelope:

Beardy Ardagh,

c/o Faber & Faber,

Bloomsbury House

74-77 Great Russell Street

London

WC1B 3DA

and write **GRuBtoWN taLes** in the bottom left-hand corner.

If you're hoping for a reply, **DON'T FORGET TO INCLUDE A STAMPED SELF-ADDRESSED ENVELOPE**. (If I had to buy all the stamps and envelopes myself, I'd probably end up having to wear the same vest for a month, and that might frighten my neighbours.) Not that I can promise you'll get a reply, of course. I may peel off the stamp and try selling it back to the Post Office.

(Just some of) the folk who pop up in GRuBtoWN taLes

Jilly Cheeter girl and one-time duck-gatherer

Mango Claptrap a short boy in short trousers, whatever the weather

Manual Org a smoothy skinned fellow

Flabby Gomez Mayor of Grubtown

Kumquat 'Grabby' Hanson the chief of police

The Grumbly girls the seven Grumbly daughters

Hacking-Cough Gomez the mayor's brother

Big Man Gomez the mayor's dead dad

Pritt Gomez the mayor's wife

Tundra Gomez the mayor's son and heir

Formal Dripping official village idiot for the
nearby village of Werty

**Derek, Bunty, Shaun, Mantle, Fastbuck &
Garrideb Fox** the duck-hating Fox family of
humans (not foxes)

Rambo Sanskrit council job-giver-outer

Sonia Pipkin local builder

The troll inhabitant of Beardy Ardagh's airing
cupboard

Mrs Awning town accident-waiting-to-happen,
first name unknown

Minty Glibb owner of Minty's Cake Shop

Mickey 'Steamroller' Johnson doughnut-
loving steamroller driver

Leggy Prune the future Mrs Johnson

Mrs Johnson the former Leggy Prune

Constable Gelatine a police sergeant

Mustard Tripwire an officer of the law and
Gelatine's nephew

Galaxy Tripwire a train driver and former
beauty queen

Relish Tripwire a tropical fish salesperson

Informative Boothe a very knowledgeable chap

Hobo Browne a gentleman of the road/smelly
tramp

Camshaft Thrift owner of The Rusty Dolphin
Cafe

Farflung Heaps self-appointed leader of an
angry mob

Garlic Hamper the lighthouse keeper

Shoona Loose the world-famous singer who
does a lot for animal charities

Tawdry Hipbone movie star

Snooks Miss Hipbone's pampered pooch

Luminous Shard bald heckler and mechanic

Carlo Monte the riverboat gambler

Lefty Scorn proprietor of Scorn's Laundrette
    & Jeweller's

Acrid Scorn an irresponsible dumper of
hazardous waste

Jip the town pelican (official mascot)

Marley Gripe a painter of signs

Dr Fraud a pretend doctor (but he's cheap)

Sloop Cheeter Jilly's dad

Harvey the Cheeter family dog

Furl Claptrap Mango's dad

Carport Claptrap Mango's mum

Vestige Claptrap Mango's brother

Claws their cat

Partial Coggs Grubtown's resident artist

Slackjaw Gumshoe paint & hardware store
owner

Purple Outing very rich owner of Purple Outing's
Music Shack

Hind-Leg Outing amongst other things, mother of
Purple's vast number of children

Wide Brim Petty-Mandrake a regular
complainer

Hetty Glue-Pen cinema manager and
projectionist

Condo Blotch former cleaner now head of her
very own keep-fit and health-food empire

Emily Blotch Condo's daughter

Free-Kick leader of the escaped lab rats

Lulu Free-Kick's mate for life

Hardfast Tendril Grubtown's chief forester

Paltry Feedback a printer and cake decorator

Careworn Wormwood nine-day king of Grubtown

Glowering Silt general manager of Fettle's hotel

Avid Folklore manager of Fettle's hotel

Chevvy Offal owner of Offal's Sunbeds

Premix Stipend victim of one of Offal's sunbeds

Pageant Conquest food-maker (and Grabby
   Hanson's sister)

Mossy Edging a very fair judge who doesn't
   take bribes that often

Hybrid Byword the (now dead) TV chef

Limbo Goulash an office worker

Clam Wretching founder of Wretching's Dairy

Barton Wretching her son and current owner of
   the dairy

Beardy Ardagh honoured citizen of Grubtown
   and the teller of these tales

The delightful Beardy Ardagh tells of other GRuBtoWN taLes

I f you want to grow up to be a healthy, happy person with LOTS OF FRIENDS, it is very important that you read all the **GRuBtoWN taLes**. Just to make sure that you've read each of those published so far – INCLUDING THIS ONE BY NOW – I've taken the time and trouble to tell you a bit about the others, over the next few pages. So CHECK THEM OUT.

Immediately.

Thank you.

Now leave me alone.

GRuBtoWN taLes
Book One

StinkiNg Rich aNd Just PlaiN StiNky

or

A Diamond As Big As His Head

Grubtown is full of oddballs – from the singing Grumbly girls to a family of duck-haters, and an outsized mayor who's knitting a new house – but Manual Org is too repulsive even for them. Getting him to leave town is top priority, until the discovery of a humongous diamond changes everything.

YOU SHOULD HAVE READ THIS ONE ALREADY!

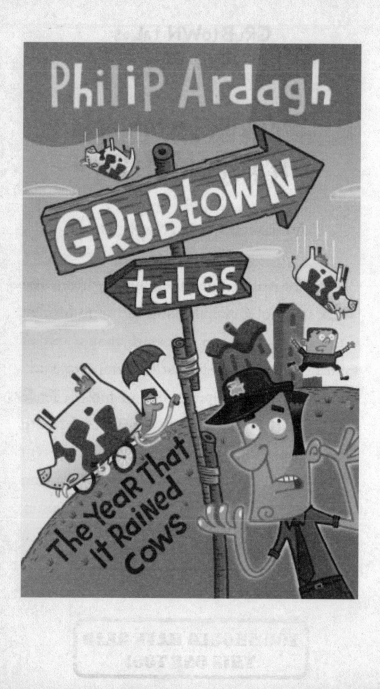

Philip Ardagh

GRuBtoWN taLes

taLes

The YeaR That It Rained Cows

GRuBtoWN taLes
Book Two

The YeaR That It RaiNed Cows

or

That Well-Known Secret Door

A startled cow falling out of nowhere onto Limbo Goulash while he's riding Marley Gripe's bicycle marks the start of a chain of events strange even by Grubtown's standards. Soon damaged property includes **PURPLE OUTING'S MUSIC SHACK** and Minty Glibb's attempt at the world's largest (strawberry) jelly-trifle. With Mayor Flabby Gomez throwing a wobbly, all chief of police, Grabby Hanson, can do is have the cow-fearing townsfolk watch the skies. Underground, meanwhile, there lies another big surprise.

YOU SHOULD HAVE READ THIS ONE TOO!

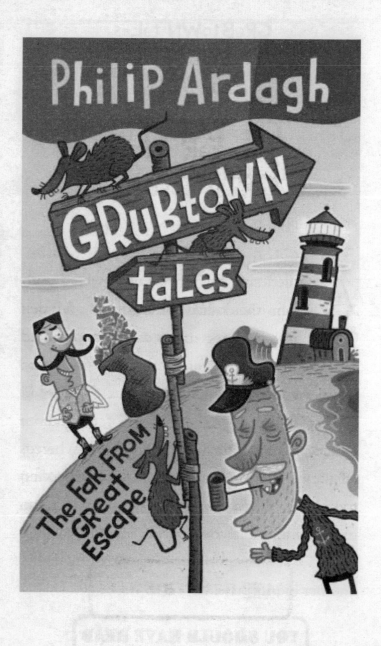

GRuBtoWN taLes
Book Three

The FaR FroM GReat EscaPe

or

The Light, the Switch and the Wardrobe

When the local lighthouse is plunged into darkness and a ship runs aground – flattening *The Rusty Dolphin* – it's hard to imagine things can get much worse in Grubtown. But then there's a jailbreak and the Police Department (all three of them) needs all the help it can get from the (often bonkers) townsfolk. No wonder more trouble is waiting just around the corner.

AND READ THIS ONE!

GRuBtoWN taLes
Book Five

TRick Eggs aNd RubbeR ChickeNs

Things all start going on the bonkers side of very wrong when Mayor Flabby Gomez finally finishes knitting his new home. He declares a public holiday in Grubtown for its official opening. There will be free ice-cream and entertainment ... only there's been a mix-up at the suppliers and the wrong costumes and props have arrived. And, if that weren't bad enough, there's the matter of a serious leak at Grubtown's new aquarium and carwash.

OUT MAY 2010!